CreativeKiDs publishing

ISBN 978-1-55454-450-9

The Princess and the Pea

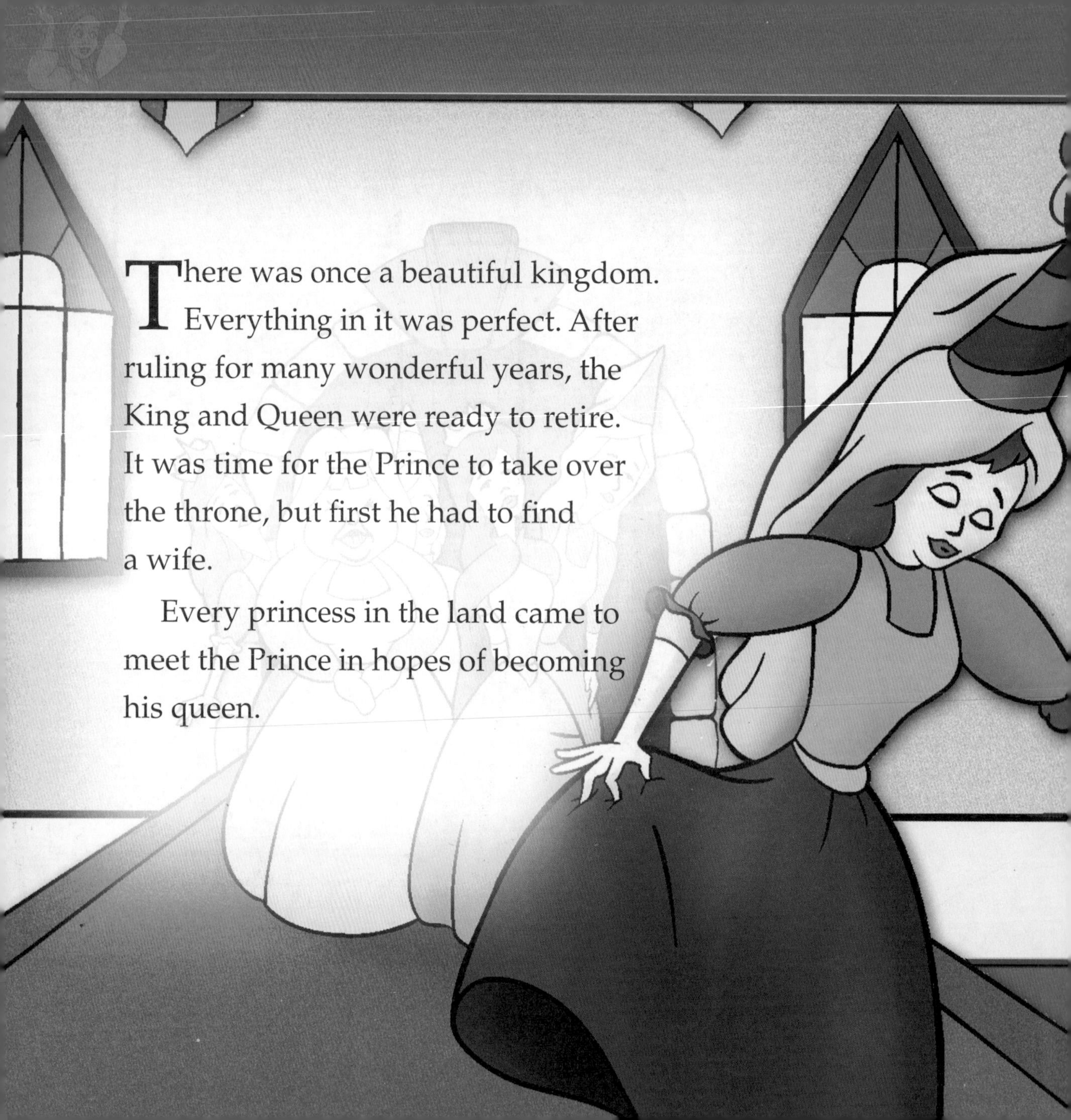

There was once a beautiful kingdom. Everything in it was perfect. After ruling for many wonderful years, the King and Queen were ready to retire. It was time for the Prince to take over the throne, but first he had to find a wife.

Every princess in the land came to meet the Prince in hopes of becoming his queen.

Many of the princesses were from the most royal of families. Although they were both beautiful and kind, the Prince could not find one of them who was just right for him.

Very unhappy at not finding his perfect princess, the Prince was ready to give up. He was certain he would spend the rest of his days alone.

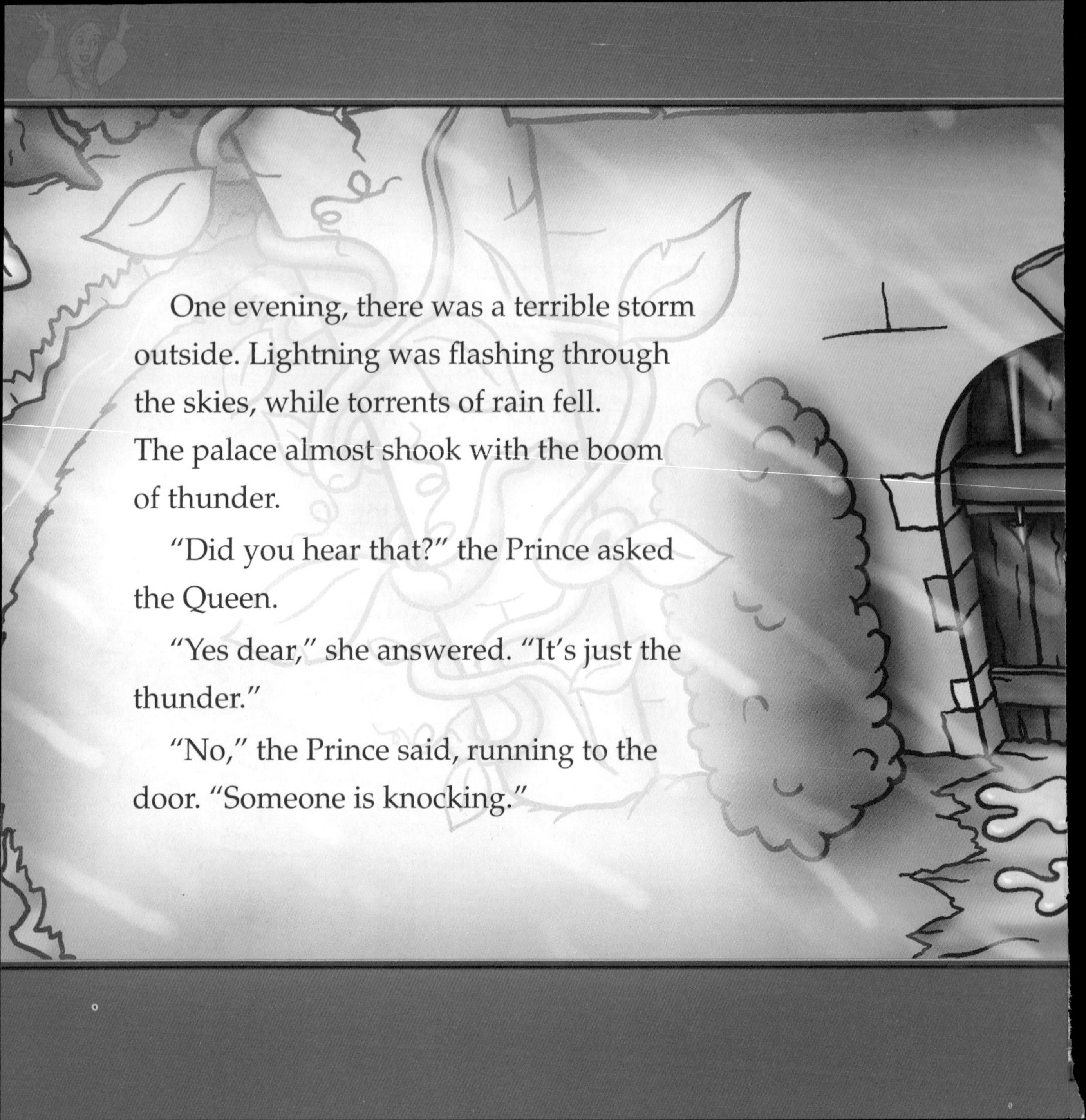

One evening, there was a terrible storm outside. Lightning was flashing through the skies, while torrents of rain fell. The palace almost shook with the boom of thunder.

"Did you hear that?" the Prince asked the Queen.

"Yes dear," she answered. "It's just the thunder."

"No," the Prince said, running to the door. "Someone is knocking."

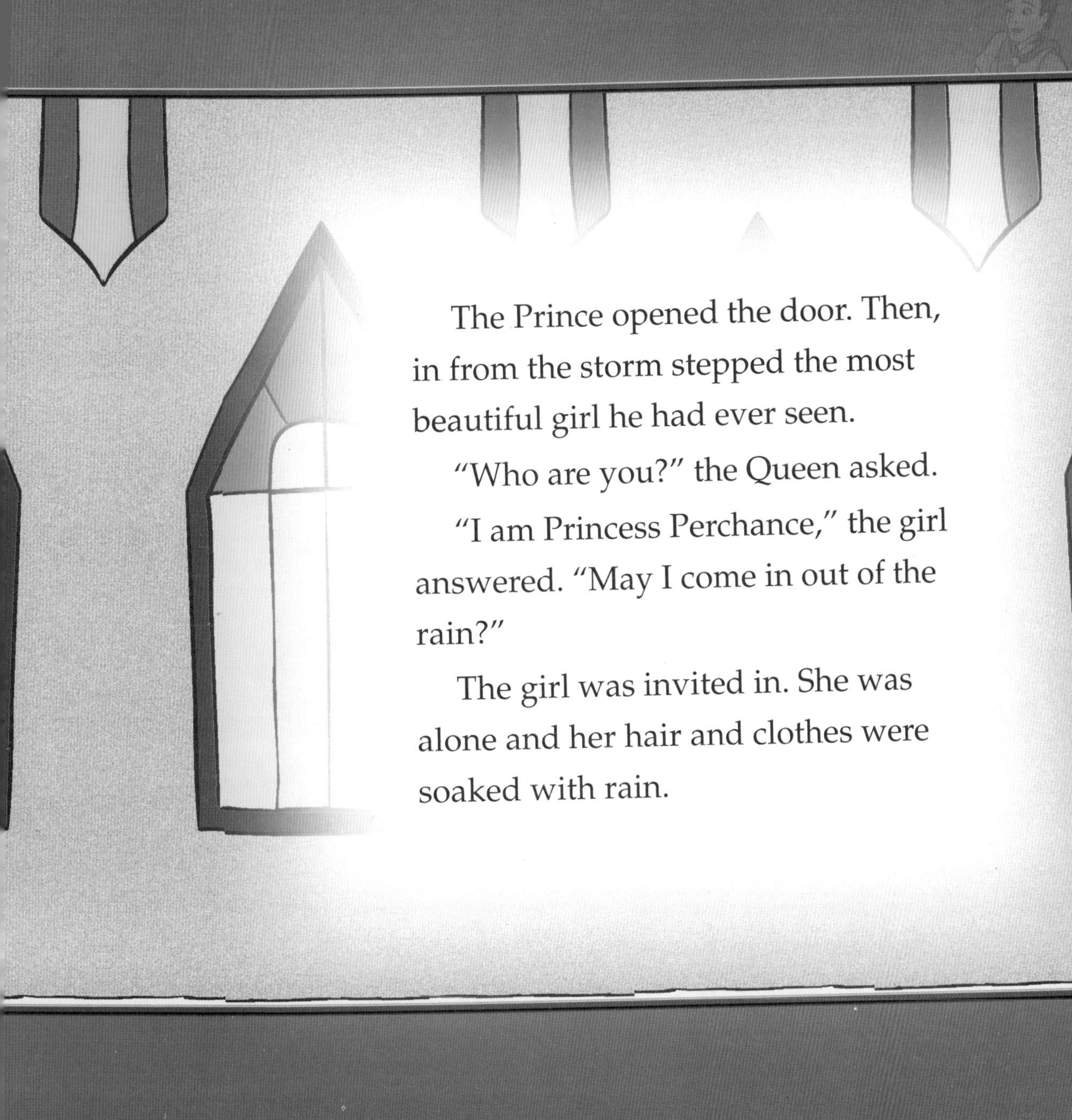

The Prince opened the door. Then, in from the storm stepped the most beautiful girl he had ever seen.

"Who are you?" the Queen asked.

"I am Princess Perchance," the girl answered. "May I come in out of the rain?"

The girl was invited in. She was alone and her hair and clothes were soaked with rain.

Princess Perchance was offered dry clothes and a delicious meal to warm her. The Prince took an instant liking to the Princess and they spent hours talking together.

"This is the one!" the Prince whispered to his mother.

"We shall see about that," the Queen answered. She didn't believe that the wet creature could really be a princess.

The Queen was determined to prove that the girl was not a princess. She had her servants make a wonderfully soft bed, six mattresses high. Underneath all the mattresses, she put three small peas.

Any regular person would think it was the most comfortable bed they had ever slept in. But a princess—a real princess—would not be able to sleep in it.

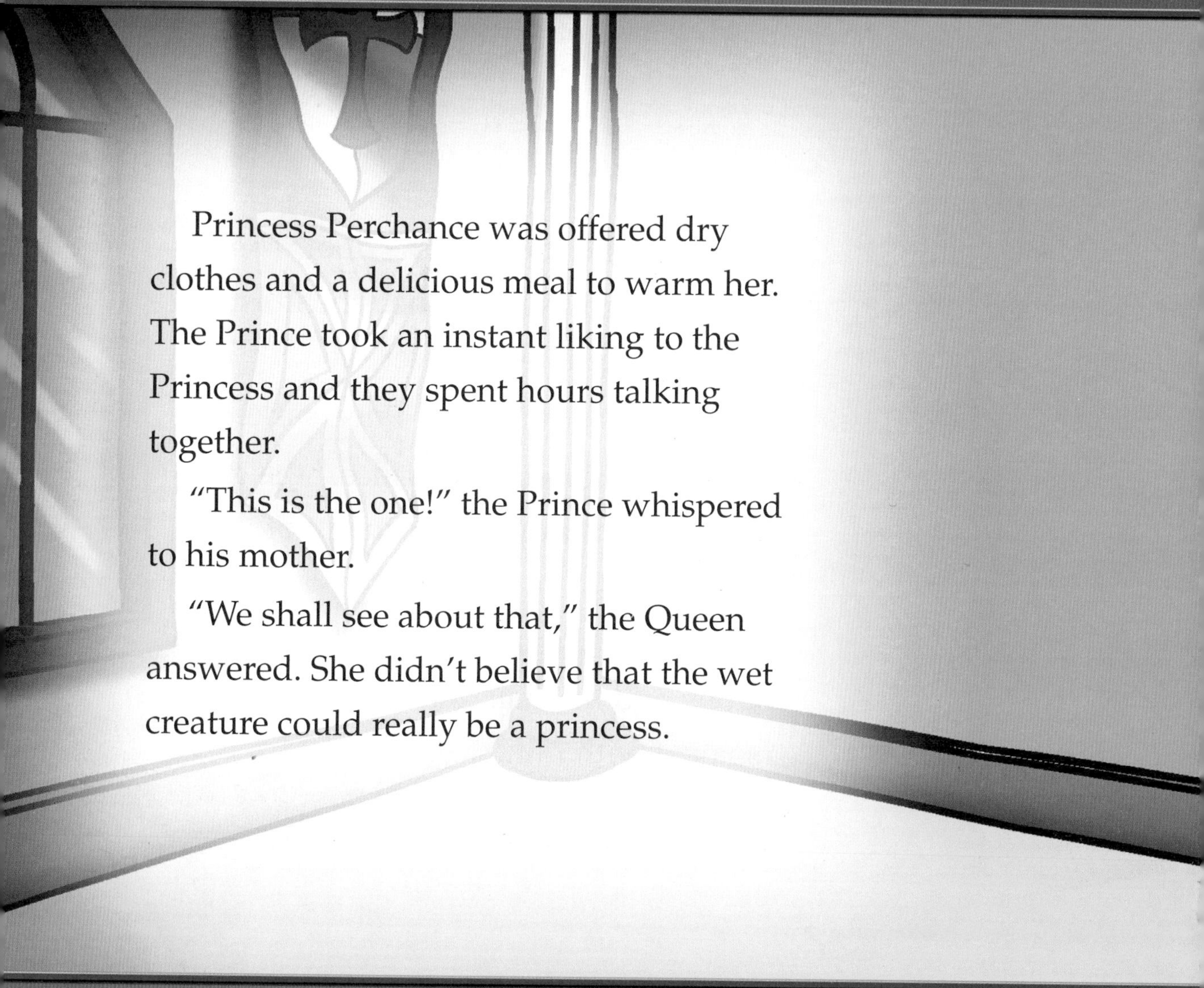

Princess Perchance was offered dry clothes and a delicious meal to warm her. The Prince took an instant liking to the Princess and they spent hours talking together.

"This is the one!" the Prince whispered to his mother.

"We shall see about that," the Queen answered. She didn't believe that the wet creature could really be a princess.

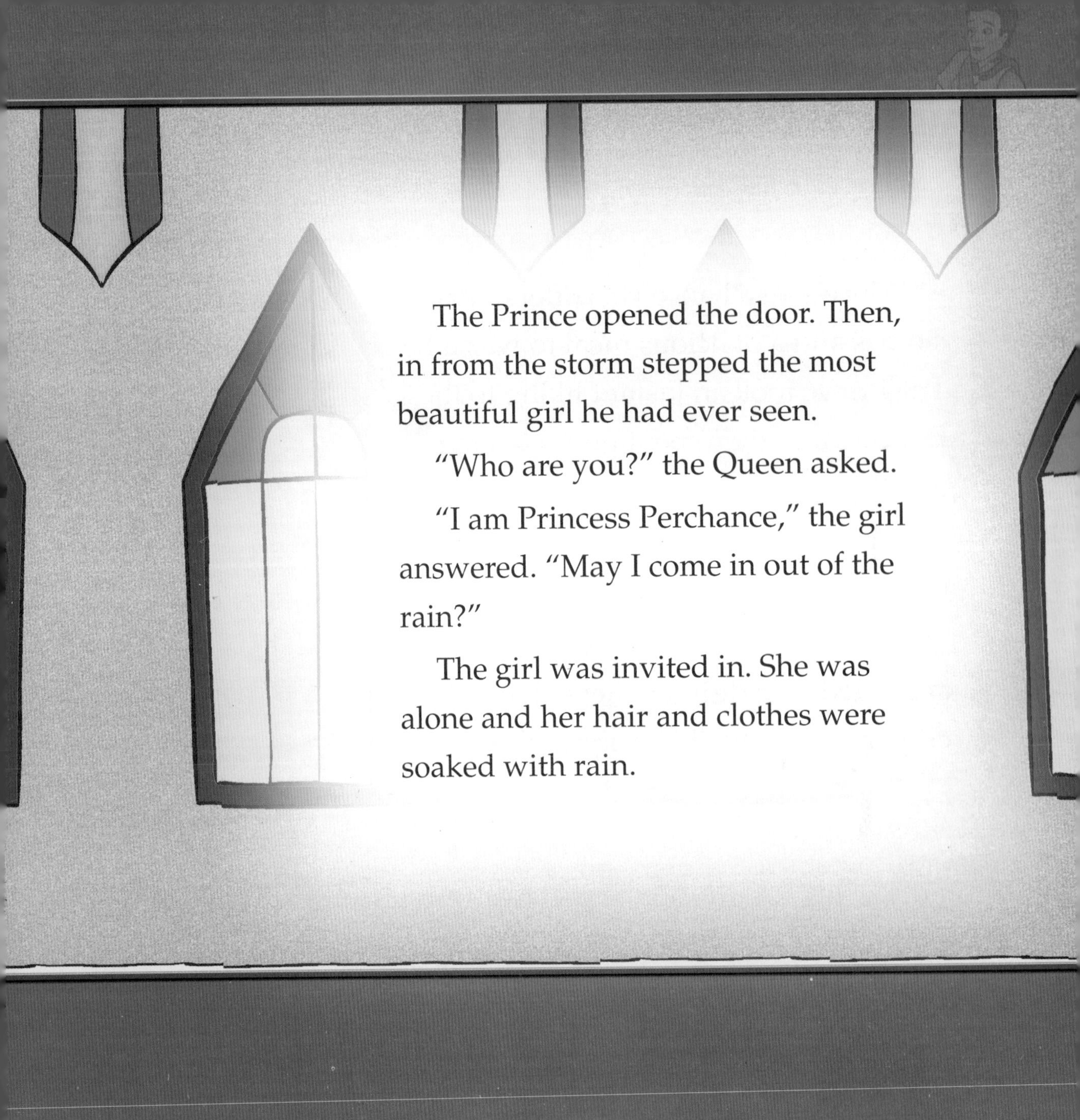

The Prince opened the door. Then, in from the storm stepped the most beautiful girl he had ever seen.

"Who are you?" the Queen asked.

"I am Princess Perchance," the girl answered. "May I come in out of the rain?"

The girl was invited in. She was alone and her hair and clothes were soaked with rain.

Princess Perchance thanked the Queen for her kindness before climbing up onto the many soft mattresses to sleep.

Morning finally came. The Prince and his mother went to see how their guest had slept. They found the girl lying way up high on the six mattresses with her back to them. The Queen was certain she had been right about her.

“There, you see,” the Queen said to her son. “This girl slept like a baby. She was not bothered at all by the bed.” The Prince was disappointed, perhaps his mother was right about the girl.

Just then, Princess Perchance sat up on the bed. She had dark circles under her eyes and looked even more tired than she had the night before.

“Princess Perchance, what’s the matter?” the Prince asked.

“I am very sorry,” the princess answered. “I don’t mean to be ungrateful, but this is the most uncomfortable bed I have ever tried to sleep on. I didn’t sleep a wink all night.”

“No princess, I am sorry,” the Prince answered with a smile. Now he knew for certain that she was a real princess.

"From now on, we will make sure you have only the most comfortable bed in the palace," the Prince told her.

The Prince had finally found the love he was searching for. They married and together ruled the kingdom very happily for many years. Once again, everything in the palace was perfect!

THE END